WALK IN THE PARK

A DCI JAMES HARDY THRILLER

JAY GILL

BOOKS BY JAY GILL

Knife & Death

Walk in the Park
(A Short Thriller)

Angels

Hard Truth

Inferno

A free bonus chapter is available for each book. For more information visit, www.jaygill.net

CHAPTER ONE

He stood and watched as the final moments of her life slipped away.

She was very pretty; much prettier than the last one. He stared at her smooth white legs. He considered covering her naked lower half but decided he no longer wanted to touch her.

You can be like that when they find you, he thought.

The hammer would need to be cleaned again. He'd need to burn his sweater and jeans. His trainers he could put in the washing machine. They were too expensive to simply throw away. And, anyway, he hated new trainers; they were ridiculously bright white when you first got them.

She was still now. No more gasping for breath. The spasms, jolts and twitches had stopped. He stared at her lifelessness for a few seconds. Fascinated.

He wondered where she might have been going. Had she been on her way home? Going to work? Or simply enjoying a walk in the park?

He stopped himself. *Don't think about it. The bitch is dead. It's over. Move on.*

Over his shoulder he could hear ducks, their wings violently flapping and pounding the water. They were fighting and making a godawful row. Eventually one of them gave up and flew away in noisy protest.

Time to go, he thought.

He walked across the grass to his bike, which lay next to the path where he'd dumped it. Lifting the bike, he leaned it against himself. He opened the pannier and dropped the hammer inside.

Without looking back, he set off for home. The challenge of getting to his room without being stopped by Mum lay ahead. She always had questions. "Where have you been? Do anything nice today? Do you need any laundry doing? What would you like for dinner?"

He'd stay in for the rest of the day. Sit with Mum, eat snacks and watch the quiz shows – she loved quiz shows. He might be on the news later.

The warm breeze felt good on his face as he picked up speed. The smell of summer filled his nostrils. The park was his favourite place; it felt like freedom.

The woman flashed across his mind. He tried to remember whether she'd said anything. With each woman it had been the same: he'd heard their noise but never precisely their words. He could guess what they were saying, but it was strange how the words became nothing more than background noise. In some ways he felt that was fortunate; he didn't need their words rattling around in his head. He wanted to remember only how each accomplishment felt.

He felt good, and he knew he'd walk with a bit of a swagger for a few days. He hoped the good feelings would last longer than last time. He wouldn't do this again. He definitely wouldn't do this again.

With a smile, he pressed on. He was feeling so energised that the pedalling was easy. Life felt good again.

He turned his face away and looked at the trees as he approached an old man walking his small copper-coloured dog.

"Come on, Sheeran, my friend," said the old man. "Forget the squirrel. Do your business and let's get home. I don't want to be out here all day; your mother will begin to worry about us."

The dog ignored him and continued to pull on his lead towards his furry nemesis.

The old man tugged the little dog, and they continued along the path they walked every day.

CHAPTER TWO

I was sitting at my favourite table in Rosie's Tea Shop. It wasn't the fanciest place in London to get breakfast, but in my opinion it was the best.

I'd been visiting Rosie's for as long as I can remember. Rosie was a close friend. Over the years we'd shared a lot. I was there for her during the dark days when she got ill and was told she needed treatment, then an operation, then more treatment. Then, a few years back, I was of comfort, I hoped, when her marriage ended.

We'd shared a lot of good times too. I'd seen her daughter, Rowena, get great exam results; get into her preferred university; fly the nest; graduate with a first-class honours degree; get a great job and move to Scotland; fall in love and marry a Scot. Most recently Rosie was giddy with the news she would soon be a grandmother.

Rosie was a friendly ear for me when my wife, Helena, was murdered. I was on my knees with heartbreak and angry with the world, but Rosie was always there for me. She probably never fully understood how much that meant to me.

To me, Rosie's Tea Shop was more than just somewhere I went to get fabulous food. It was a place I often brought my family to and meet friends at.

"I think we were lucky to get a table. It's really busy this morning," said Monica.

Monica was my wife's best friend, and when her violent marriage had forced her to leave her home, my late wife insisted she stay with us. She still had a room with us.

"Shall I make sure they haven't forgotten us?" We could see the girls were getting irritable.

"I'm hungry," said Faith for what felt like the hundredth time. "We've been waiting ages. Mr Puppy's hungry too. He hardly ever says that, so he must be *really* hungry." Faith started spinning her favourite toy, Mr Puppy, around and around on the table.

"You're such a moaner," said Alice. "And Mr Puppy doesn't have a mouth or an appetite or any kind of digestive system. He's not real."

Faith swept up Mr Puppy and held him close. "Daddy, can you tell her? Did you hear what Alice said? Tell her."

I looked at Alice, my eldest daughter, in a way that showed my disapproval.

"Here comes Rosie with our breakfasts now," I said with more than a little relief.

"Here we are – two orders of pancakes with summer fruits and chocolate sauce for my two favourite girls."

Rosie slid the plates in front of Alice and Faith. Their eyes widened on seeing the mountains of pancakes. Rosie then disappeared for a moment before returning with two more plates. "And two full English breakfasts."

"Thank you, Rosie. I think you just saved two little girls from starvation. These two have been acting like they haven't eaten in a week."

Faith scrunched her nose at me, and Alice gave me one of the scathing looks she'd been perfecting. I pulled a face straight back at her.

"We were just saying how busy it is this morning," said Monica. "I guess we're not the only ones who love your weekend specials."

"I know. It's great, isn't it?" Rosie sighed and looked around. "This was not the morning for my precious goddaughter to decide to skip work."

I noted more than a hint of frustration.

"Where is Ceri?" asked Alice. "She always makes us laugh."

Faith looked up at Rosie now, her mouth bulging with pancake.

"I don't know where she is, sweetheart. I guess she stayed with a friend last night. A sort of sleepover," said Rosie. She looked at Monica and me and continued. "I'm cross because she didn't call to let me know. Also disappointed she's left me short-staffed this morning. Let's just say she and I will be having some serious words when she shows her face. She's a sweet girl, but she's a bit of handful." Rosie winked at Faith.

"I don't envy you," said Monica. "I remember what I was like at nineteen."

"Cover your ears girls," I joked. Monica gave me a playful dig in the ribs.

"Don't even go there," said Rosie. "Attitudes have changed a lot since I was her age. I'm wondering if I've taken on more than I can handle. I am worried. I feel so responsible for her."

"Bit of a party girl?" said Monica.

"You can say that again. She's confident enough, but I think she's perhaps a little naive. Coming from such a small hometown, she's just not that streetwise."

"I'm sure James will have a word with her."

I nearly choked on my toast. Monica gave me a couple of slaps on the back. After a sip of coffee, I said, "Of course. Better than that, I'd be happy to take her out in a patrol car on a Friday night to see all the scumbags causing misery. That'd be a reality check for her."

Rosie laughed. "I'm not sure it's come to that, but if I can't talk sense into her I'll let you know."

"I'm serious. Just give me the word," I said.

"Thank you, James. I'll leave you to your breakfast. If there's anything else I can get you, just let me or one of the waitresses know."

"Thank you, and good luck," said Monica with a chuckle.

Rosie winked at Alice and Faith then went back to helping her waiting staff.

Faith swallowed a mouthful of pancake. "Daddy, can I come with you to see the scumbags?"

Alice groaned, and Monica covered her mouth in an effort to stifle her laughter.

"Maybe when you're a little older, sweetheart," I suggested.

"What are scumbags?" added Faith.

"Okay, Faith, how about you finish up those pancakes before they get cold?"

I looked at Monica, who was now wiping away tears of laughter.

"You're not helping. You're supposed to be an adult," I said with a grin.

CHAPTER THREE

After breakfast the girls wanted to look around the shops. I was keen to walk off some of the calories and agreed to join them.

We arrived at a large Marks & Spencer store and, rather than do lots of walking, my role became one of giving my opinion on a range of different outfits.

Alice and Faith were growing so fast, and it had been a while since they'd been shopping with me. This was a good opportunity to get them some new outfits. I did my best to help, but when it came to clothes for the girls, Monica really came into her own.

"What do you think?" said Alice. "This would be good for Brianna's party."

"Do you like these shoes?" said Faith. "I like the sequins on the front of this sweater. Can you see it's a kitten? Can I get it?" She started marching in some high heels Monica had tried on.

"You know, I like them all," I said, feeling more than a little out of my depth. "Let's see what Monica thinks."

Monica opened the door to her changing room and stepped out. She had on a long tight-fitting summer dress. She looked in the tall mirror and held up her hair. She looked stunning. My heart started working overtime, and I swallowed hard.

She looked over and I looked away, pretending I'd been looking elsewhere. *We're friends, nothing more, and that's how it has to be.*

I tried to stay casual. I cleared my throat. "That's nice. That really suits you. You'll knock 'em dead in that. You should get it. My treat."

"I don't know. I think it's a little tight under the arms." She turned her attention to Alice and Faith, who were looking on with curiosity. "Well, look at you two. I love that kitten top, Faith. Not the shoes so much. And Alice, that is so pretty. Perfect for the party. You know, I've seen some nice slip-ons that'll go really well with that."

Watching the girls enjoying themselves, I couldn't help thinking that, in spite of everything we'd been through, I was one hell of a lucky guy.

My phone rang. I reached inside my jacket and pulled it out. It was my boss, Chief Webster. Everyone knew it was my day off and, guessing it wouldn't be anything important, I went ahead and answered it.

I should have known better. When would I ever learn?

CHAPTER FOUR

"James, I'm sorry to bother you on your day off."

"Unless someone's dead, I'm sure it can wait until Monday." Webster's tone of voice told me he was under pressure, but I was annoyed at him for intruding on my family time and even more annoyed with myself for answering the phone in the first place.

"Someone *is* dead. Another young woman in Regent's Park," he said.

I felt the excitement of the day drain away. Out of the corner of my eye, I saw Monica's disappointment at realising the family day had ended.

I wanted to hang up. I wanted to turn back time and not answer the phone. The other part of me, the police officer, took over. "When did it happen?"

"She was murdered yesterday. Member of the public found her this morning. This is the second young woman found in the park in two weeks. You know what this means."

He didn't need to spell it out. Officially, a serial killer

commits three or more murders, but two women turning up dead, two weeks apart in the same park, meant the chances were high there would be a third, and soon. By calling me, he was letting me know he was taking the threat seriously and felt another death was now only a matter of time. Webster wanted me on the case sooner rather than later.

"How can I help?"

"I want you to support the two lead detectives. Offer insight. Work with them. Do what you do. Stop this bastard before he does it again."

"Where's the body now?" I shuddered. The thought of another innocent life, violently snatched away, made me go cold.

"She's on her way to the morgue. Heidi Hamilton is on scene. She'll head up the post mortem."

Hamilton was the department's forensic pathologist. "Good. Okay. I'll finish up here. I'll be there in a couple of hours."

"Sooner the better. I just got off the phone with the mayor. It's the height of the holiday season – I don't need to tell you how many tourists visit the park. This is giving him all sorts of headaches – all sorts of headaches he's all too keen to lay at my door."

"Jerk," I said. Webster made no comment. "Who are the lead detectives?"

"DI Fuller and DS Jensen. Good homicide detectives, but neither has handled a serial killer investigation before. Work with them, help them."

"I'll be there as soon as I can." I'd almost forgotten I was with my family. I glanced across and watched them holding up various pieces of clothing and asking one another's opinion. Monica had noticed me turn my head and looked back at me, concern on her face.

"And Hardy?"

I was about to hang up. My mind was racing, preparing itself for the myriad of questions that lay ahead.

"This killer is a particularly vicious piece of work."

CHAPTER FIVE

Detective Inspector Fuller was loud and energetic. He was a short, slightly overweight man whose narrow eyes, balding hairline and ill-fitting suit made him look older than his fifty-six years. He scratched inside his nostril with his little finger then passed me a coffee.

"Here she is. This is DS Jensen. The sergeant here will go through the files with you." Jensen stood a few inches taller than Fuller and her attractive appearance, engaging smile and relaxed demeanour were a welcome contrast to Fuller's intensity.

"Nice to meet you, sir. I've heard a lot about you and read even more." She blushed a little and was clearly kicking herself for sounding like a fan. I pretended not to notice.

"Let's go through what you know so far; bring me up to speed."

Jensen opened the thickest file and started describing the first case while I listened and studied the photos.

"The first victim is Julia Moore. Newly married

and worked part-time as a junior accountant. She was attacked while out walking her baby. Baby had difficulty sleeping during the day, so either she or her husband would take it out in the pram. Baby's crying is what attracted a passerby to the scene of the attack."

The photos were tough to look at. Moore was partially clothed, and the number of repeated blows to right side of her head made her facial features barely recognisable.

"When did this attack occur?" I asked.

"Two weeks ago. Friday the seventh. We're pretty certain the attack took place between nine thirty and ten a.m."

"Where?"

"Regent's Park. Next to the boating lake. He somehow got her off the path. We think he must have threatened her or threatened to harm the baby. Either that or he grabbed her and dragged her."

Jensen's face reddened. She said, "I know it's all sounding less than conclusive."

"You're doing great. Keep going," I said.

Jensen nodded and continued. "I have a theory she knew she was going to be raped and led him away from her baby. Her instincts would have told her to get him as far away from the child as possible."

"She just never expected him to then beat her death," added Fuller. "She took a gamble."

There was a lot of uncertainty. I would have expected them to have answers after two weeks, but I said nothing. I hadn't been there at the outset of this investigation, so I couldn't pass judgement. It didn't stop me feeling frustration, though.

Jensen passed me what little they had on the most recent murder.

"Can you get me a copy of both case files?" I asked her, keeping my voice even. "Everything you have. Everything. I want to get up to speed as quickly as possible, and that'll mean going over everything again. Some of which I'll do at home."

"Of course, sir."

"Thank you. And please, you can stop calling me 'sir.' Call me Hardy."

"Yes, sir." Jensen looked at Fuller, who shrugged. Jensen pointed to the second file now. "This is the second victim. This took place yesterday, in all likelihood, mid-morning. We're waiting to get the pathologist's report to confirm that. But it means the attacks are roughly two weeks apart," said Jensen

Fuller took over. "Regent's Park again. Not far from the first attack. This time right next to the bandstand. Same MO. Raped and beaten to death. Looks like the same weapon was used, probably a claw hammer."

Jensen pulled out the crime scene photos and started placing them down one at a time in front of me.

"We're waiting for a formal identification. Her family are on their way from Wales," said Jensen. "However, she did have some identification, and so we think her name is—"

"Cerise Williams," I whispered. The words came out, but I couldn't believe I was saying them.

CHAPTER SIX

How could this be? I picked up the photos again. There was no doubt. I went cold. My mind felt like it'd been hit by a tornado. My mouth was dry.

"Cerise Williams," I repeated. "Rosie's goddaughter."

"You know her?" asked Fuller.

I was silent. I was having difficulty comprehending what my eyes were seeing and what my brain was telling me. How could these sickening images be of the same sweet young woman who had only a week ago chatted so attentively with my little daughters? They'd been so excited by the attention and so disappointed when she wasn't there again this morning at breakfast. I wanted to rage and swear and curse God.

I took a long trembling breath and said, "Yes, I know her. Her name *is* Cerise Williams, but she liked to be called Ceri. She is the goddaughter of a very dear friend."

I wondered how I was ever going to break the news to Rosie. I knew I'd be breaking her heart forever.

"How sure are you?" said Fuller.

I looked at him and he took a step back, then muttered something about updating Chief Webster. Jensen waited for him to leave.

"I'm truly sorry, Hardy," she said gently. "Would you like me to leave you alone for a while?"

I took a breath and tried to focus. However much I was hurting, there was work to be done. I owed it to Ceri and to Julia Moore to catch the sick bastard who had done this to them.

"Carry on. You're doing great. I want to know everything," I said and nodded encouragingly.

From what I'd seen of her, Jensen was a very capable detective sergeant, and she understood that right now we had to put all emotion aside. The anguish I was feeling was unbearable, and I was fighting hard to hold back tears. The shock of seeing someone I cared for end up murdered in this way was unbearable. Yet, no matter how much I wanted to express my rage, it would have to wait. There would be time enough later to face the heartache. Right now, I had to hold it together and do my job.

We spent a good couple of hours going over the files and bouncing questions and scenarios back and forth. I was keen to ensure I knew as much as Fuller and Jensen did, and Jensen was keen to understand my perspective and glean early insights into the type of man I thought was responsible.

Jensen said, "The press has started calling him the

Regent's Park Ripper. Pretty sick, I know. On top of that, the mayor's giving Chief Webster a hard time. I guess that's why he called you in. To help us, I mean. And hopefully before this guy does it again." We were both aware of the pressure that put us all under.

"You've done a great job so far. Everything you tell me makes sense," I said. "The crime scenes were handled as I would have expected. We've collected DNA evidence from the victims. But what we don't have are suspects. And if our killer isn't in the DNA database, then DNA is no good until we have a suspect. We're a long way from catching this guy."

"What do we do next?" asked Jensen.

"I need to discuss that with Fuller. This is his case," I said diplomatically.

Keen as I was to take the lead, this was Fuller's investigation and I wasn't about to step on his toes. I had been brought in to advise, and that was what I would do – in theory, at least. Jensen looked like she was about to say something but changed her mind.

She rubbed her eyes.

"The best thing you can do right now is to get something to eat then go home and get some rest," I told her. "You're no good to anyone if you can't think straight. I promise I've been where you are right now, and even though it feels counterintuitive, sleep really is your friend. I'm going to take the copy files and study them at home. I'll probably have some questions in the morning."

Jensen handed me my duplicate case files. "Our mobile numbers are on the insides of both files, in case you need to reach us. Call me day or night. I'm not much of a sleeper."

"You might regret that offer," I said, trying to muster a smile.

"I want this killer off the streets more than anyone else I've investigated," said Jensen. "And with only a two-week window until he kills again, I feel like the countdown has already begun. I don't want to waste a second."

"The countdown has begun, and if he waits another two weeks to kill again, I'll be very surprised."

Jensen looked shocked.

"I'll know more tomorrow," I said. "Get some rest."

CHAPTER SEVEN

One of the worst parts of a police officer's job was telling a stranger that someone close to them – a child, a partner, a parent, a friend – had been snatched from them, that someone they cherish beyond words had been snuffed out in a violent way.

It was almost unbearable when the person you were telling was a friend.

Rosie had closed up and as usual was working late on getting things ready for the following day. I'd deliberately waited until the cafe was closed. I took a deep breath then tapped on the glass of the front door.

From behind a table Rosie looked up at me and waved. "We're closed – come back tomorrow," she joked, loud enough for me to hear.

She unlocked the door and welcomed me in. "Not that it's not always lovely to see you, but don't you have a home to go to?"

She closed and locked the door behind me. Out of habit, she checked the 'Closed' sign was the right way around. When I didn't answer, she turned and looked at me. "You look like hell, James. Are you okay?"

I forced out the words I couldn't let anyone else say. "Rosie, I'm so sorry. I'm here about Ceri. She—"

Rosie knew instinctively what I was about to say. Something – a look in my eye, maybe – told her I was about to deliver the worst news she could ever hear.

"Don't you say it, James. Don't you dare tell me it's her. Not her, not that sweet child. You can't come here and tell me this." Her legs buckled and I reached out to catch her. She slid to the floor next to the counter.

I sat beside her and held her hand. "I'm sorry, Rosie, so deeply sorry. I saw her myself. There's no doubt."

We held each other, cried and talked. Rosie told me about Ceri's movements over the last few days and weeks. People she'd met, friends she'd made. Her relationship with her parents and Ceri's need to break free from the small Welsh town she'd grown up in and find herself. It was the same coming-of-age story that had been told a thousand times before, but for Cerise Williams it had ended tragically.

"I suppose if you're asking all these questions, you don't know who did it?" asked Rosie finally. She got to her feet, went to the back of the Tea Shop and returned with a half-bottle of single malt. She poured us each a large glass.

"Not yet," I said honestly.

"Do you think you ever will?" Rosie drank hers down in one and poured herself another. "I'm sorry, I shouldn't have said it like that. I know you're hurting as much as I am."

"I'm going to get whoever did this. You have my word. Whoever is responsible will pay."

Rosie said nothing. The pain was too much to say anything else right now. Instead, we sat together and finished the bottle of whisky.

CHAPTER EIGHT

Accompanied by a large pot of strong coffee, I spent the rest of the evening and most of the night working through the case files, doing all I could to know as much about the murders as Fuller and Jensen did.

Eventually, exhaustion caught up with me and I fell asleep in my big old comfy chair. During the night Monica must have checked on me and, rather than disturb me, put the case files aside and covered me with a blanket. She was a good friend.

The sound of Alice and Faith getting ready for school drew me to the kitchen.

"Morning, Daddy," said Faith.

"Morning, Daddy," said Alice. "Did you fall asleep in the ugly chair again?"

They looked at me disapprovingly.

"Morning, girls. I may have done. It's my thinking chair; it's not ugly. It won't happen again."

"That's what you said last time," said Alice.

"You don't think in it – you sleep in it," said Faith.

"It *is* ugly. Mummy always said it was ugly, and she was right."

I looked to Monica for support without success.

"You've got me there – I give in. That's exactly what Mummy always said. Give me five minutes and I'll take you to school." The girls broke into whoops of delight, which made me smile.

I retreated to the shower, and thirty minutes later we were outside the school gates. The girls bundled out of the car, and I stepped out to the kerb with them, kissed them both, and hugged them a little tighter than usual. "Work hard, you two. Listen to your teachers, but don't forget to find—"

"Don't forget to find the fun," said Alice.

"You tell us that every day," said Faith. "Find the fun, find the fun."

I pulled a face and growled like a bear. "Are you telling me I sound like a broken record? Get out of here." The girls giggled and disappeared inside.

It didn't take long before my mind returned to Ceri and thoughts of how eventually I'd have to break the news to Alice and Faith. I headed back to my car, where I looked at the two case files on the passenger seat. I took a deep breath and headed to Regent's Park.

Moving between Julia Moore's crime scene and Ceri's, I began looking for similarities. Location-wise, they were both large, open spaces, which meant the attacks had been daring. There was some tree cover where Moore's attack had taken place, but there was quite a distance between the path she would have walked and the trees where her body was discovered.

Ceri's body had been found between a bandstand and a large weeping willow tree. Once again, a path ran alongside and there was an open grassy area.

Choosing these locations for the attacks meant that the killer had taken quite a gamble. It was possible that the risk of being discovered was part of his sick game, but he must have felt comfortable enough with his surroundings to know he was safe.

That must mean he knows the park, I thought. And if he knows the park, then there is a better than average chance he lives locally. I wondered if he had spent time studying Moore. We knew she frequently used the park to push her baby.

Ceri, on the other hand, wasn't local. She lived with Rosie, and that was at least a thirty-minute bus ride away. He couldn't have studied her. That meant the attack on her had probably been spontaneous.

The lack of planning, the open location, the spontaneity of the second attack, the element of daring, the bravado and the brutality, along with the killer's choice of weapon, all made me think the attacker was young, somewhere between twenty and thirty-five, maybe forty at a push. I felt sure an older male would take less risk.

Think, Hardy, I told myself. *To catch this killer, you have to think like him.*

Why here, and why them?

CHAPTER NINE

He laced up his trainers and put on a new sweater. The bag under the bed caught his eye. The contents needed to go in the incinerator. *I'll do it tonight*, he said to himself. He kicked the bag under the bed and out of sight.

He could hear Mum in the kitchen. Could he get out of the front door without speaking to her? Was that mean?

He simply couldn't face going through the whole 'gratitude' thing again today. He looked at himself in the mirror. Another year older. He put his middle finger up at himself, and the world, and forced his anger through it. He added the finger on the other hand. They wouldn't catch him: he was too smart.

Halfway down the stairs she heard him.

"Morning, sleepyhead. You almost slept your birthday away." His mother rushed over and gave him a tight squeeze and a kiss. "You're never too old for one of my special hugs."

"I guess not," he said. He pulled away when she started tidying his hair with her fingers. "Mum?"

"Come into the kitchen and I'll dish up your breakfast. I suppose it's brunch now, judging by the time. Come on."

"Nah, I gotta go. Maybe later."

"Don't be silly. Come on, for your mum. I don't see you that much. You're always out. Always working. It's Sunday. It's your birthday."

She had a delicate nature, which, to a certain degree, had been her downfall. She was one of those people who were too trusting and too easily taken advantage of by others.

He smiled and gave her a kiss.

"Goody-good," she said.

He sat at the table while she fussed around him. As the eggs fried she put a mug of tea down. "Nice and milky, with one sugar," she said. "Just how you like it."

"Perfect."

"My big boy – look at you. All grown up. You're a man now. I remember when you were tiny, probably only four or five, and you used to fly up and down the pavement out there. Do you remember? On that blue bike of yours? You never bothered with stabilisers. You jumped on and away you went. All day you'd be out there. Up and down, up and down. Those were the days."

"You mean the days before Dad fucked off with that slut-bitch of his."

Mum's smile turned to pain.

"Sorry," he said. "Sorry, Mum." *What an idiot.* He studied her face.

But nothing was going to spoil today. She carried on buzzing about like he'd said nothing. She slid the eggs onto his plate and put the full English breakfast down. "The bacon should be nice and crispy, just how you like it. Burnt to a crisp, I call it." She laughed.

He squirted on some tomato sauce. The toast popped up in the toaster, and Mum buttered it before sliding that in front of him, followed by a couple of presents.

She sat down opposite and beamed.

"Thanks, Mum. You didn't need to."

"Yes, I did. I'm your mother. If I can't spoil you, then who can? It's not every day Mum's baby boy turns twenty-six. I want to make each day count. One of these days some fine young woman will catch your eye and that'll be it – you'll be gone. So I'm going to spoil you." She dabbed her eyes.

"Oh, Mum, don't cry. I ain't leaving. I'm staying right here. I'm going to look after you. Remember? It's you and me. The dynamic duo." He got up and gave her a hug. He passed her some kitchen roll.

She wiped her nose. "I'm a silly cow, I know. I'm sorry. I'm spoiling your brunch. Come on, eat up."

"You're not silly. Don't put yourself down. You're amazing. Look at what you've done for me. And I don't just mean this morning." He tried to make her laugh.

She smiled and put her hands either side of his face and gently squeezed. "Thank you, sweetheart. I just wish—"

"I know. It's his loss. The bitch turned his head and that was it. He was weak."

"And stupid," she said, wiping away the tears.

"Exactly."

"It's harder on birthdays and at Christmas."

"We're all right."

"Yeah, we are, aren't we?" She tucked the kitchen roll in her sleeve and sat up straight. "Don't let it get cold. Eat up. I want to see you open your presents."

"This is good, Mum. The sausages are lovely."

"They're just cheap ones."

"They're nice."

"I'll get my phone. I want to take some pictures of you."

"Really?"

"Yes, really. Mums like having photos. It's one of the things that make us mums." She disappeared into the other room and he looked at the clock.

He was keen to get to the park and take a look. He couldn't leave her, not yet. He'd go out later. Run an errand of some kind and at the same time pass by. He felt sure the place would be swarming with police. He wanted to see.

"Smile. Come on, give me a big birthday smile. That's better."

"All done?"

"You are an old grump, you know. You take a good picture. You're very handsome. You should have a girl, you know." She started looking at the pictures and showing him.

"What about that girl from college? What was her name? Polly, Pippa?"

"Poppy." He felt himself flush with tension. "She was nothing."

She turned her back to him and plugged in her phone. "That's a shame. She seemed lovely." She paused then said, "You're a man. And I know a man has needs. Mrs Schumann can help. We could call it a birthday treat."

"For Christ's sake, Mum. Can we not talk about this? I'm eating my breakfast."

"Okay, but I understand. I do. And she only keeps, you know, clean girls. I just don't want you taking any chances. She said you're always welcome."

He put down his knife and fork. "You talked to her about me?"

"Not really. I just bumped into her at the chemist and I mentioned your upcoming birthday." Recognising her unintentional play on words, she tried to hide her smile.

He stared at his breakfast. "Can we please change the subject? I don't need Mrs Schumann or her tarts."

"Of course," she said. "Just so long as you're sure."

"I'm sure." He started eating again, then, shaking his head, said, "Mrs Schumann? What are you like?"

After a moment's silence they both burst out laughing.

"'She only keeps clean girls,'" he said, mimicking his mother's voice.

CHAPTER TEN

With only two victims from which to build the killer's narrative, I knew it would be hard to pin down his motive. The sad truth is, the more victims, the easier it is to find important similarities between them and get closer to the killer himself.

In cases like these, I usually started with the victims and why a killer would choose them. Often, a victim's appearance or personality type played a role in why they were chosen.

In the case of Ceri and Julia's killer, I wondered if he went out with the intention of killing a young woman, *any* young woman? Did they look at him the wrong way? Did they speak to him? How had he approached them? Why did he choose them over all of the other women who must have been in the area at the same time? Why did he feel the need to not only rape them but kill them? And why so brutally? The attacks had been ferocious, and this killer's choice of weapon showed he wanted to inflict maximum damage. It wasn't enough to just kill them; he rained down blow after blow after blow. Why did he hate them? Who or what did they represent to him?

Think, Hardy. There were two major crimes here. Rape and murder.

But … what if this wasn't about the sexual attack? Maybe this was about the killing. That would make sense. That might be why DNA samples collected from the victims didn't match any offenders in the DNA database. Rapists often work up to their crime over time; they're often found to have committed crimes likes public indecency first. The sexual aspect of Julia's and Ceri's murders was perhaps a further humiliation he wanted to inflict on his victims rather than his primary motivation.

Flashes of the crime scene were mixed in my head with memories of Ceri's smiling face. I could see her crouched beside Alice and Faith listening to their stories. Stroking Mr Puppy's ear while Faith asked her about Wales and her parents and family.

I looked around. My eyes followed the edge of the lake to a huge willow tree, then to the bandstand where Ceri was found. I turned and could see more large trees. Tall grass. Shrubs. Oak trees. Large expanses of lawn. Paths weaving through it all.

Out of nowhere a cyclist whizzed past me ringing his bell furiously. I stepped sideways to get out his way and nearly fell. I held up my hand to apologise. I'd been miles away and hadn't seen his approach.

I hadn't seen him approach. *I hadn't seen him approach.*

I took off at a run towards the willow tree, then ran

from one crime scene to the other, praying I would find what I was looking for. I took photos on my phone and compared them. The grass was disturbed the same way at each scene.

"He approached on a bike. They hadn't seen him until it was too late," I said to myself out loud. "He dropped the bike and went straight at them. He as good as came out of nowhere. He shocked them, then attacked."

I looked up and down the path. I paced up and down, furiously trying to picture what had happened.

"You approached from the front. Casually getting a closer look. But you didn't stop. You cycled past. You kept going. You knew the way was clear from your approach, so you continued past to check the coast was clear from behind. Satisfied, you turned around and then came straight back at them from behind."

I raced home and locked myself away in my study. I furiously made notes and drawings. Piecing together what I'd learned. From what I knew now, could I build a picture of the killer? I needed to build a solid profile I could put to Fuller and Jensen.

As soon as I had enough I called Fuller's mobile phone. He didn't pick up. I immediately dialled Jensen's number.

"Jensen. I need to meet with you and Fuller, straight away. I've built a profile, and from that we can narrow down the search. It'll save days."

Jensen stopped me. "Haven't you heard? We have him in custody. He came in and confessed. He's with Fuller now."

I sat back in my chair. "What? That doesn't make any sense." The idea he'd hand himself in knocked me sideways. I looked at my notes. Something didn't fit.

"I'm sorry, Hardy. It's been crazy here. I thought Fuller told you."

"Forget that. How old is your suspect?"

"Give me a second." There was a long silence while Jensen went to find out. "He's sixty-two."

"I'm coming straight over. Tell Fuller he's not your man."

"What?"

"Just tell him."

CHAPTER ELEVEN

I met Jensen outside the interview room. Fuller was sitting with the suspect going over his statement.

We watched on monitors. The suspect looked frail and nervous; I could see his hands trembling as he turned and slowly read each page of his statement.

"Tell me what happened," I said. "Who is this guy?"

"His name's Peter Richards. He's a widower who lives alone just outside Maidenhead. He's a retired financial advisor; specialised in pension plans.

"Fuller got a call this morning from the front desk to say Richards wanted to see him. Richards told the front desk he had evidence on the Regent's Park Ripper investigation. Once he got upstairs to us he said he'd murdered Julia and Cerise. Fuller showed him into the interview room, and he's been with him on and off all day."

I watched as Richards took out a handkerchief from his pocket and wiped his glasses. Having signed the statement, he took off the glasses and tucked them inside his jacket pocket. Was this really our killer?

Having taken DNA samples from Richards, we'd have to wait a couple of days at least for DNA comparison results to come back. Meanwhile, the real killer could be preparing to attack again. We needed a way for Richards to rule himself out of the investigation or, if he really was our man, rule himself in.

"You don't look convinced," said Jensen.

I was pretty sure Jensen had doubts herself, but she would follow her superior's lead.

I didn't want to rain on Fuller's parade. I'd already sampled his temper, and we needed to work as a team. It was important I didn't make him feel stupid. But time was short.

"Does he look to you like the man who overpowered Julia and Ceri?" I asked Jensen.

"He might look like a weak old man but sometimes you never know."

I got to my feet. The investigation didn't have time for this. I knocked and waited for Fuller to excuse himself.

Fuller looked delighted with himself as he closed the door to the interview room. He held up the statement.

"It all seems to fit," he said. "He's confessed to the two attacks. When I pressed him he admitted three other earlier sexual assaults. He claims it's only recently he's felt the need to kill. He's a deeply troubled man. He claims his dark side has been growing for decades, but since his wife passed away four years back he no longer feels the same compulsion to restrain it."

Fuller put his hand on my shoulder. "Jensen mentioned your doubts, but she's young and she's learning. We both know sometimes we get lucky and things fall into place. Today was one of those days. Be happy – we've got all we need right here." He waved the statement. "I guess you can go back to working your own cases. We didn't need Scotland Yard's greatest psycho-killer detective after all."

Beside me, I heard Jensen clear her throat and could feel her shift uncomfortably.

I wasn't sure what was going on with Fuller. He seemed to have a massive chip on his shoulder about something, and perhaps one day he and I could talk about it, but right now wasn't the time.

"He's not our guy," I said bluntly.

Fuller looked at us both. "What the hell are you talking about? He confessed."

"I can see that, and I don't know why he confessed, but the killer is still out there and we need to catch him."

Fuller looked at Jensen, who shrugged and said, "I'm young. I'm learning. You said it yourself."

CHAPTER TWELVE

"Listen to what I've got to say, then decide whether to go to Webster," I said. I was trying to prevent Fuller from making a fool of himself, but he couldn't see it. He looked uneasy. Finally, he nodded in agreement.

"Attacks of this kind point to a younger man," I began, "somewhere in the region of twenty to forty. That's based on the ferocity of the attack and the way the victims were beaten to death. I also believe the killer lives locally; he knows the park. He knows the busy times and the quiet times. He knows places he can observe users of the park without being noticed."

"Is that it?" scoffed Fuller.

"You really think Richards drove all the way from Maidenhead to Regent's Park to attack these women? What's that, a sixty-minute drive?"

"Probably more, the way traffic usually moves on the M4," remarked Jensen.

"There is no reason to think he didn't drive there to do exactly what he said he did," said Fuller. "And if you've got nothing else, I'm going to take this statement and give it to Webster. I'm sure the chief will be delighted the case is closed."

"I've got plenty more, but there isn't time. We need to get Richards to eliminate himself from the enquiry so we can move on."

Fuller looked at me blankly. "How do you propose we do that?"

"With some proper police work. Jensen here is going to ask Richards some questions about the murders and the crime scenes. I'm guessing he'll give you an answer to them all. Even the made-up ones."

I turned to Jensen and said, "Ask Richards why he bit the victims and why he put coins in their mouths."

Fuller said, "There were no bites or coins?"

"Exactly," I said. "Only the real killer will know that."

Jensen went back into the room, and we stood outside watching her and Richards. Fuller looked seriously pissed off. I didn't care.

After no more than twenty minutes she rejoined us.

"I guess you heard all that?" said Jensen.

"Every word," I said.

"When I asked him about the bite marks, he hesitated but then took no time coming up with a reason for doing it. Same with the coins left in their mouth. He had answers for everything. He even went on to tell us how he strangled them. Which is bizarre, given that earlier he explained how he'd used a wrench to bludgeon them."

"He wanted to please you," I said. "It's not

uncommon. What did you make of his manner when you confronted him about the false questions?"

"That's when he broke down and started crying. As you heard, his obsessions and fantasies about young boys are overwhelming him. He claims he's never actually followed them through. But he's scared he will and wants to be arrested. He wants help."

Hearing all this, Fuller finally lost his cool. "This is bullshit," he said. "The guy's a fucking loser, and he's just wasted my day on his depraved fantasies." He kicked over a chair. "I'm going to get some air. Jensen, deal with that loser. Get somebody down here who can get him help – whatever *that* looks like. Just get that animal out of my interview room."

It wasn't pretty, but I'd got the result we needed. Richards had ruled himself out.

"He'll calm down; he just needs to walk it off," said Jensen, looking in Fuller's direction. "He gets like that sometimes. He takes things very personally. Deep down he's a good guy."

"How deep?" I joked.

"Deep, very deep," Jensen said, laughing.

"Fuller wanted it to be Richards and that's what Richards used," I said, trying to sound sympathetic and not quite succeeding.

"So, what now?" asked Jensen.

"We go after our man by building a profile from what we know."

Jensen looked excited. "Let's get some coffee and go to work."

CHAPTER THIRTEEN

Jensen handed me a coffee. She also put one down for Fuller, who had spent the last hour with Chief Webster. He'd calmed down and apologised for losing his cool.

No apology was needed. We all wanted the killer off the streets, and with the clock ticking we were all feeling tense. That sort of pressure we each handled in our own way.

The clock on the wall loomed over us unnervingly.

"I don't want to bring a downer on our position, but it does feel like we're back at square one," said Fuller.

"I have to agree, Hardy," Jensen told me. "It feels like we should be out there, doing something."

I finished putting my notes in order. "Hardly," I said. "From what you've given me I've been able to put together a profile of our man. Without this, we're going out half-cocked." I pointed to my scribbled notes. "This is the key to bringing him down."

I could see scepticism in their eyes. I wasn't used to justifying my approach to anyone, and this was why

Webster rarely partnered me up with anyone. He and I both understood I worked best alone. But I could see that this time I needed to play nice. Although it all appeared perfectly logical to me, I hoped that by patiently explaining my findings – a combination of my own psychological profiling plus the evidence the others had gathered – I could convince Jensen and Fuller to get on board.

"Let's have it," said Fuller. He and Jensen opened their note pads and began to write as I spoke.

"The spontaneous nature of the attacks and the high level of risk he was prepared to take indicates a young male," I said. "I'm sure we'd all agree, an extremely angry individual. Something or someone has caused him a lot of resentment. His anger may have started years ago but has now reached a point where it can't be contained any longer. Apart from bringing the weapon, neither attack showed a sign of the murderer having done any planning. A lack of finesse before, during and after the crime suggests low to average IQ – there's no sign that he made any attempt to cover up his crime. Quite the opposite, in fact: there is a possibility he may have taken a degree of pleasure in knowing there would be shock felt by those discovering the bodies.

"He knows Regent's Park well; that would indicate he's local. He has most likely spent a lot of time there over the years, especially his adolescent years. He feels comfortable in the park, possibly watching people and fantasising about how it would feel committing the murders. It's unlikely he would have picked a park the size of Regent's Park without knowing the exits and the many routes around it; he wouldn't have wanted to get lost after the attacks. The park might have meaning or relevance to him, or maybe its great expanse simply offered opportunity."

I looked at Fuller and Jensen, and they seemed to be following my thought process, which buoyed me.

"If he works at all, it will most likely be a manual job. He most likely lives at home with his parents. The sexual aspect of each attack suggests he's unlikely to have had much success forming personal relationships. Sexual relationships will have been a particular problem. He's probably been rejected more than once, which he finds difficult to manage emotionally."

Jensen looked up from her notes. "Lives locally and at home?"

"Relationships will have been a real problem," I repeated. "He's detached from the rest of society. I feel there is a strong possibility he lives at home. Outside the home environment he'll be a loner."

"Why couldn't this be an older man, someone in their fifties?"

"The pattern of behaviour doesn't fit. Older males will be more cautious. Their crimes are more orchestrated and more sophisticated. Certainly less risky. Yes, they can still be horrific in nature, but the spontaneity of these two crimes along with everything else suggests to me a younger man."

Jensen and Fuller looked up and both sighed heavily.

"Holy shit," said Fuller eventually. "You got all this from photos and case files?"

Jensen smiled. She looked almost giddy with enthusiasm.

"There's something else," I said. "I believe he approached the women on a bike." I pulled up the photos on my phone. "Look here, where the ground has been disturbed. That's the end of the handle bar, that's where the pedal hit the ground, and that – those are tyre marks. I've got Forensics looking at it."

"That's how he approached and got away so quickly," said Fuller.

"Nobody really takes much notice of someone on a bike. Other cyclists might offer a nod, and pedestrians simply move out of the way."

We stood in silence for a moment as we absorbed the information.

"That's going to help," said Fuller, who was all smiles. "Chief Webster has all but signed off on running a surveillance operation in the park. We just need a female volunteer to play the bait." Fuller looked at Jensen and winked.

I checked my watch and started for the door. "I'm not so sure that's the best way forward," I said. "Let's talk when I get back. I need to go and see someone who I hope can throw more light on all this."

"Can't make any promises," Fuller called after me.

CHAPTER FOURTEEN

I'd learned from experience that there was sometimes more to an autopsy report than was actually put down on the page. As with all detective work, the forensic pathologist would have insights and feelings they couldn't explain.

"You owe me dinner," said Hamilton without looking up from her desk.

"Do you say that to every detective who walks through your door?" I laughed.

"No, James. Only you." She looked up and smiled broadly. "It's good to see you. I'm just sad it's under these circumstances. I heard – I'm sorry."

"Thank you, Heidi."

"It was no way for anyone's life to end, especially one so young."

"She was a sweet girl." There was an ornate teapot on the corner of Hamilton's desk, and I found myself absently staring at it.

"Green tea?" Hamilton gestured to the pot. I could

smell the delicate fragrance.

"I'm okay, thank you. I was just thinking. A few things are trying to click into place."

"I guess you're here because you read my reports?"

I nodded.

"When I saw the second body, I thought it wouldn't be long before they pulled you in on the case. I said to myself, *I hope they get James on the team.* They'd better get this under control, and quick."

"Seems you and Chief Webster think alike. Anyway, that's why I'm here. You're a part of my team. You know I can't do my job without you. I want to know what you think."

"Flattery, always flattery." Hamilton sipped her tea. "Clear that chair. Move the papers down on the floor there. Take a seat."

She grabbed her copy of the reports and we went over them page by page. "You know the facts," she began. "Rape. Massive impact to the back of the skull. No signs of struggle."

"They're the facts," I said.

"You want me to paint you a picture?"

"Yes," I said. Although my heart was screaming no.

"He attacked them from behind with a blunt instrument of some kind. Most likely a regular hammer. He knocked them to the ground. Then, as they were dying or dead, he raped them. Then to be completely sure they were dead, he hit them repeatedly, to the point where their skulls were just pieces."

Hard as it was, I had to picture Julia Moore and

Ceri in the park suffering as they had. It made me almost physically ill. I asked reluctantly, "Anything else?"

"There was no sign of struggle. If it helps in any way, James, I would say your friend never knew a thing. Neither of them knew anything. The speed of the attack and level of violence saw to that."

"Thank you, Heidi. I truly appreciate all you've done. As soon as this is all over, I'll buy you dinner. You and me and the best bottle of wine."

"Yeah, right. You just catch this bastard. Then we'll talk about how you can repay me. I'm now thinking dinner, wine and a West End show."

CHAPTER FIFTEEN

He wheeled his bike to the tree line and dropped it beside a large row of shrubs. Opening his rucksack, he took out his binoculars, cheese-and-pickle sandwiches and a bottle of lemonade.

After last time, he'd promised himself he wouldn't do this again. Then he'd told himself there was no harm in looking. Trouble was, he knew all too well what looking could lead to.

He put the binoculars to his eyes and let his hand rummage around for a sandwich. Retrieving a square from the silver foil, he took a bite and continued scanning the park.

Nope; jogger. Nope; dude in a suit, walking weirdly. Nope; boyfriend and girlfriend. Nope; group of mums with kids in buggies.

He sighed and lowered his binoculars. He shoved another sandwich in his mouth and took a swig of lemonade to make the bread soggy.

This was bad idea. He needed to stop. He'd already

gone too far. He'd only meant to do it once. Now it was all he could think about. He checked his rucksack for a packet of crisps he knew full well he hadn't brought. He wondered whether three was a better number to stop at. Three was a lucky number. Everyone knew that.

He'd spent a lot of time considering what part gave him the most pleasure. At first, he had thought it was doing something no one else dared.

Then, after the first one, he'd thought it was the sexual part of the attack but, having given that some thought, he'd realised it had meant nothing to him. It was nothing more than a way of degrading her further. Showing her how meaningless she was.

He put the last square of sandwich in his mouth and returned to scanning the park.

No, it was after the second one. It had come to him when he was in the back garden washing the hammer. That was when he understood about the feeling of power it gave him. Power was why he wanted to do it again. Knowing they had seen him, really seen him. They might have wanted to ignore him but they couldn't. Given half a chance they'd have pleasantly smiled his way, just to be polite, and then moved on with whatever they had set out to do. If he hadn't intervened, he would have remained insignificant.

His whole life had been a repeating pattern of abandonment, rejection, failure and fear. The only constant thing in his life was Mum. And that also filled him with fear: what if something happened to her?

He took a gulp of lemonade and leaned back on the grass. Looking up at the sky, he considered his options.

What if he did it one more time? After all, the first two had been very easy.

The papers had started calling him the Regent's Park Ripper. He probably had fans who were expecting an encore. There was no denying how good it would feel to get the hat-trick, the treble. After that he could assess the situation. He'd lie low for a while then start thinking about how he could improve things for Mum. To be fair, things had been just as hard for her as they had for him.

Slinging the rucksack on his back, he climbed onto his bike and pushed hard for home. He'd get things prepared and sleep on it. Things would seem clearer tomorrow.

CHAPTER SIXTEEN

He shut the door behind him and looked over the balcony. The coast was clear. Pulling his hood up, he shoved his hands in his pockets and headed for the stairwell. He listened. Satisfied, he started down. He took the steps one by one, tiptoeing, left-right-left-right, to get down them as fast as he could.

At the bottom he looked left and right and then bounded across the grass, over the wall and onto the pavement. The shop was just around the next corner. He wanted to get back as quickly as possible. Even better if he could do it without incident.

"I need my lotto tickets, and get me a couple of scratch cards at the same time. Would you do that for me?" she'd said.

He had known it was coming, but his heart had sunk all the same.

"Could you also get a steak and kidney pie for dinner? Does that sound nice? And don't forget the milk. I've put the money by the door. I'm going to lie down for a bit. I've got one of my migraines coming on. You won't forget, will you?"

No point telling her the lottery was money down the drain; he'd be wasting his breath. They'd had that conversation too many times before.

He could see the offy and the coast was clear. Everyone called it the offy because it sold cheap booze. In reality it was more of a mini-supermarket. He couldn't remember a time when he couldn't find what he needed right there in that shop. It was better when he was a kid and Mr Mason ran it, but he'd had a stroke and had to retire. Now some Indian fella ran it, and he'd never bothered to ask him his name. He was always friendly and smiling, but you didn't talk to him. Everyone knew that.

He put the pie and milk on the counter and handed over Mum's lotto numbers. It was the Indian's daughter today. He stole a look at her. Pretty, very pretty.

"How's your mum?" she said fondly. "Please tell her Snita says hello."

"She's all right. Yeah, I will."

She handed him the tickets and put the pie and milk in a bag. "Your mum's a lovely lady. She talks about you a lot. I'm Snita. We went to same school. I was a couple of years lower—"

He opened his mouth to say something but nothing came out. He flushed and could feel himself burning up. She wasn't being friendly, he could see that now: she was laughing at him. He grabbed the bag off the counter, knocking a charity collection tin on the floor, and rushed for the door. He turned and looked back, hesitated, then decided to leave it. The door slammed and rattled shut behind him. He stood on the pavement letting the outside air cool him down.

"Virgin," yelled a voice. "Vir-gin, what you do-ing? Are you shop-ping for your mum-my? 'Ere – look that this, Virgin is out doin' Mumsy's shopping."

He didn't need to look. The voice was Brando's.

He pulled up his hood again, shoulders hunched. He'd brave it out. He'd ignore them and say nothing until he got home. He thought of the two women. He was no virgin, but he wouldn't tell them that. They were his, all his.

Brando tugged hard on his dog's lead, some sort of Staffy-pit bull mix, allowing it to get close then yanking it back while it barked and snarled at him. He let it get extra close and then had to jump out of the way of its snapping teeth. This caused Brando, and the two slags he was with, to laugh and cheer.

"Loser weirdo," called the girl he knew as Shaz. "Frightened of a dog?"

"Freakoid," spat the girl called Jez. "Such a freak."

He shut their voices out and picked up the pace. He wound the shopping bag around his hand so he could run without it swinging. Behind him the dog barked and the heckling continued.

He could see home now. He welcomed the feeling of relief, knowing he'd soon be safely inside.

He took the stairs two at a time and, before reaching the top, started rooting around in his pocket for the front door key. Never looking back, he slid the key into the lock. Closing the door behind him, he leaned against it before sliding down to the floor. He rested and focused on controlling his breathing. His hands were trembling. He thumped the floor, then thumped it harder, again and again.

"Fuck."

"That you?" called his mum. "Did you get the lotto ticket?"

Screw the lotto, he thought. Instead he said, his voice shaky, "Yes, Mum. I got it all."

CHAPTER SEVENTEEN

I got home to find Alice on her new smartphone and Faith perched next to her.

"I hope you haven't been on that thing too long," I said. "It'll suck all the goodness out of that pretty little brain of yours."

Faith looked horrified.

"Ignore him," said Alice. "It won't do that. He's just being grumpy."

I gave the girls a squeeze and a kiss on the head. "Five more minutes. Please do something else. Like pick up a book, maybe?"

I heard the girls groan as I entered the kitchen.

Mum was at the kitchen table reading the paper and enjoying a glass of ice-cold white wine.

"Something smells good," I said, opening the oven door.

"Monica's made shepherd's pie. She'll be back shortly. She's gone to get some bits for the girls' lunch boxes for school."

I could feel Mum's eyes on me as I grabbed a beer from the fridge. I topped up her wine glass and sat down opposite her. "And Dad?" I asked.

"He's out tonight. Some golfing dinner. Not my sort of thing. He's picking me up afterward. So long as he remembers."

I took a long sip of beer and loosened my tie then undid my top button.

"Tough day?" asked Mum.

"The worst kind."

"Want to talk?"

"Not really."

"You know I've heard it all before. Your dad saw it all in his day. The good, the bad and the downright evil. There's nothing new under the sun, as they say."

I squeezed the back of my neck and put the cold bottle to my forehead. "I can't say right now; it would be wrong."

Mum closed the newspaper and slid it in front of me. "Anything to do with this?"

The paper's headline read REGENT'S PARK RIPPER KILLS 2ND WOMAN. WHY?

I nodded. I couldn't tell her more, so I kept my answer vague. "Yeah. It's to do with that. Worse still, I knew her. She was a sweet girl. Very young. She was simply in the wrong place at the wrong time."

"I'm sorry, James. Like I've said so many times before, we need more bobbies on the beat, but instead there are cutbacks. And that puts pressure on those that remain. Look at you. You look like you're ready to drop. You can't keep this up indefinitely."

"Not now, Mum. It's been a long day. Even with more officers, he would have found a way. They always have and they always will."

Mum tutted. I could see she wanted to say more, but for my sake she didn't.

Monica arrived back with two bulging shopping bags. Alice and Faith raced to help her before I could get to my feet. They started checking the bags for goodies while conferring and lining up the treats on the work top.

"Hi, Mon," I said. "You okay?"

"Yep, all good. Starving, but good." She could sense the dark cloud hanging over us. "Are you two okay?"

I didn't want Alice and Faith to hear anything, so I pointed discreetly to the newspaper headline.

"Okay," she mouthed silently. "Maybe later."

It had been a few days since I'd been able to sit down for an evening meal with everyone, and I'd missed it. The mood lightened once the food was on the table and the conversation turned to what was going on at school with Alice and Faith. Their adventures soon had us all laughing and joking and sharing our own stories, which, for a while, made us forget about the darker side of life.

CHAPTER EIGHTEEN

Jensen had changed out of her uniform and was now looking more casual. The clothes transformed her. They were similar to those worn by Ceri, and it was hoped this would trigger a response in the killer. It was a dangerous game, as we were all well aware of how that response could look.

"Okay, she's ready. Let's get this show on the road," said Fuller as Jensen disappeared into the ladies' changing room again. "We have a green light from the boss. Let's see if we can catch ourselves a fish."

I didn't like Fuller's implication that Jensen was bait and we were trying to catch some small fish. This guy was no fish; he was a predatory shark. My other problem was Fuller's assumption that by simply dangling a line in the water we'd get a bite. I wanted to take a more proactive approach.

"Let's delay the operation," I said to Fuller, making sure Jensen was out of earshot.

"What? Are you kidding? Do you have any idea how hard it was to get Webster to sign off on this?"

"I think I do. And I'm not saying we don't do it. I'm suggesting we hold off until we've pursued other avenues first."

"Come on, let's not go over this again. Sitting around hoping for a result on the sex offenders register is a waste of time. You said yourself it's a long shot."

"Then the other option is that we go door-to-door," I said.

"You're kidding, right? Do you know how long that will take? You said yourself that we don't have much time. You said the clock is ticking. How many officers do you think we'd need to canvas the homes around the Regent's Park area? Forget it. Our best option is for him to come to us. If we're going to catch the Regent's Park Ripper, we have to draw him out and catch him in the act."

"The level of violence he's prepared to inflict makes this approach dangerous."

"Jensen's a big girl; she's smart and she can handle herself. And we've got more than enough officers for this kind of surveillance. She will be monitored at all times. We've even got some spotty-kid officer flying a drone overhead."

Jensen heard her name mentioned and joined us. "What am I missing?" she asked.

I kept quiet. The worst thing I could do was introduce doubt into her mind; she needed to remain sharp.

Fuller raised a hand to me in a way that said "Go on – you tell her she's in danger."

"We were just discussing which area of the park to focus on first. It's a big park."

"The Regent's Park, as it is officially known, is 166 acres, which is roughly equivalent to 111 football pitches," Jensen said, as though reciting at school. "It contains Regent's University London and the London Zoo. As well as several public gardens and some formal gardens, there's a lake and an open-air theatre. There is also the Regent's Canal, which runs through the northern end of the park and connects the Grand Union Canal to the London docks."

Fuller laughed and slapped my shoulder. "I told you she's smart. Now, Jensen, what have I told you about spending too much time on Wikipedia? You need to get out more."

I kept my expression neutral. I was less and less crazy about the idea, but I could see Fuller's point and I had to remember this wasn't my case. I could voice my concerns but, in the end, I had been brought in to advise.

Although I tried to hide it, Jensen could see the concern on my face. "I'm all right with this," she said. "I volunteered, remember? And anyway, you've got my back, right?"

I didn't find her air of confidence convincing. It was apparent neither of us was completely happy with Fuller's decision. All I could do now was be a part of the team and ensure every step possible was taken to ensure Jensen's safety.

"Damn right. If anyone even looks in your direction, you'll know about it. You have my word."

"In that case, what are we waiting for? Let's do it."

Jensen was as tough as any detective I'd known, and tougher than some. She was also smart enough to be scared, but there was no way on earth she was going to let anyone there sense it.

CHAPTER NINETEEN

We couldn't have undercover officers on the ground walking close by. The operation depended on the Regent's Park Ripper believing Jensen was a vulnerable woman out by herself using the park. We were setting a trap for a predatory killer who was picking off those weaker than he in an ambush-style attack.

Instead, we had to make sure Jensen was forewarned of anyone approaching so she could protect herself until help arrived.

She was a well-trained officer, and she was wearing a lightweight stab vest under her sweater. She was carrying pepper spray and had a taser tucked inside her handbag. But I knew that her knowing self-defence and combat techniques would do her no good if she was knocked unconscious by an unexpected blow from behind.

We were monitoring Jensen as she walked the chosen route. It passed the locations of the two earlier attacks and seemed like the logical point at which to start the operation. I could only imagine what was going through Jensen's head each time she approached the crime scenes.

The park was full of open space, and for the operation to be convincing there could be no sign of anyone else around when the Ripper approached.

We were close by, but not too close; it would take nearly a minute and half for any officer to get to her. In that time Jensen was on her own and would need to defend herself. To say I wasn't happy was an understatement.

For two days, we had nothing. Each day was excruciating, as we couldn't let our guard down for a second.

"How are we doing, team?" Jensen asked us via her microphone on the evening of the second day. "You've got eyes on me, right? You haven't popped out for pizza, I hope?"

Jensen was heading in the direction of the bandstand, close to where Ceri had been murdered.

"We've got you, Jensen. Our eyes haven't left you for a second. Just one thing," said Fuller.

"What's that?"

"We finished the pizza and we've moved onto the blueberry cheesecake. It's bloody lovely too." Fuller and a couple of junior officers started laughing hard.

"Screw you, Fuller. You're such an idiot," said Jensen.

"We're all here," I said. "The same couple you saw

earlier with a little girl on a tricycle will be with you again in a couple of minutes." I checked my watch. It was getting late and the light was starting to fade. I looked at Fuller and he nodded. "Make your way back carefully to your car. That's it for today. We're losing light, fast. We'll go again in the morning."

"Suits me fine. I'm freezing my butt off out here. Maybe tomorrow I could wear a nice thick jacket and some trainers?"

"The clothes are similar to those worn by Cerise," I told her again.

"You don't need to remind me. The difference is I'm not nineteen anymore, and these heels are killing my bloody feet." She started to laugh a little, and I sensed she was feeling the relief of safely getting to the end of another day.

Everyone was feeling the same. After long hours of nothing, the tension had built up until it was unbearable.

I could see Jensen from the surveillance van. It was a dark-green and gold park-maintenance van parked close to the lake. "I've got eyes on you, Jensen, You're all clear. Just a few hundred yards now. Go straight to your car and we'll follow you out. Stay in character. He might be studying you."

I turned to the two junior officers who were now chatting. "This operation isn't over until she's back safe. You got it?" I snapped.

I turned back to the window and raised my binoculars again. I'd only looked away for a second. Out of nowhere a cyclist had appeared and was closing fast on Jensen's position.

"Who's that?" I shouted. "Behind you, Jensen."

"What? Where?" Jensen turned and tightened her grip on the pepper spray. It all happened so fast. Jensen stepped aside and prepared herself as the cyclist approached.

Fuller was on his feet. "I can't see his face. He's wearing some sort of mask over his nose and mouth."

Everyone held their breath. I had my hand on the van's sliding door.

"You okay, Jensen?" I asked.

The cyclist looked at Jensen, thanked her for moving aside and sailed past.

"Yeah. All good. But I need a drink. And it had better be a double. What a day. What a bloody day."

CHAPTER TWENTY

Outside the park the cyclist was stopped and questioned. We were all exhausted and feeling jumpy. We sat in silence waiting to hear whether this was our man.

"Negative," came a voice over radio. "He's not our man."

"How certain?" Fuller pushed back.

"Well, sir, he's a she. The cyclist is female," replied the officer flatly.

"Fine. We're calling it a day," said Fuller.

Everyone was frustrated. We'd all put in a long day with nothing to show for it. The operation might not have yielded any results, but it had run smoothly and Fuller had gone up in my estimations. He might be tightly wound and a hard man to deal with, but he knew how to run an operation and was surprisingly well respected. I realised I might have misjudged him.

Fuller's mobile phone started buzzing on the desk in front of him. Then so did mine.

"Detective Hardy," I said. The voice on the other end sounded anxious.

"Sir, there's been another attack. On the other side of the park. Behind the tennis courts, near the running track."

Jensen arrived just as I was climbing out of the van. "You're coming with me to the hospital," I said, passing her the bag containing her change of clothes. "I'll explain everything in the car. You can change while I drive."

CHAPTER TWENTY-ONE

We left Fuller to wrap things up at Regent's Park and raced straight to the hospital.

"We're here to see Catherine Simmons," I told a junior doctor as we entered the emergency room. Jensen and I held up our warrant cards. "It's important we see her immediately."

The young doctor looked confused and, being unsure what do, made a phone call. "Follow me," she said finally.

"How is she, physically?" I asked as we walked. I needed to ascertain the extent of the attack she'd suffered.

"When she arrived, Mrs Simmons was very shaken. Understandably so. Physically, she is okay. We treated her for some minor scratches and abrasions. Emotionally, not so good. She was swinging from being tearful to hysterical. I think it's the shock. We've given her something to calm her nerves, so she might appear a little drowsy.

"You can see her for a few minutes, but she must rest. My name is Doctor Li. My shift ends in about an hour, but please ask for me if I can be of any assistance."

"Thank you, Doctor Li," said Jensen as she pushed open the door to Catherine's room.

The doctor introduced us, and for a while Catherine ignored us. I let Jensen take the lead, feeling that was the right way to go.

"My husband?" said Catherine eventually.

"He's on his way, Mrs Simmons," said Jensen. "As soon as he gets here, the nurses are going to bring him to you. I promise."

"Would you mind if we ask you a few questions about what happened? While we wait for your husband," I asked gently. "It's really important we catch the man who did this to you."

"It was him, wasn't it?" asked Catherine.

"Him?" said Jensen.

"The so-called Regent's Park Ripper."

"We don't know at this stage. Perhaps you can tell us what happened? If it is him, you might be able to help us catch him and save someone's life," said Jensen.

Catherine looked at Jensen. I could see in her eyes she was gathering her thoughts, trying to put in order the events that had led up to her lying in that hospital bed. Surprisingly, she smiled broadly.

"I beat the crap out of him and he ran away," said Catherine.

"Good on you," said Jensen encouragingly.

"As soon as I felt the shove from behind I knew what

was happening. I felt this huge push and I was knocked off balance. Somehow, I guessed it was him. I'd seen a report on the news of those poor women. At the time, I said to myself that if he came after me I'd fight back – and I did."

"You're a brave woman," I said. "Without a doubt it saved your life."

Jensen sat down next to Catherine and passed her a tissue that she held onto but didn't use.

"I hit the ground hard. Straight down on my face I went." She touched her cheek and winced. "I knew what I had to do. I saw it on YouTube ages ago. A self-defence video. I got to my feet as quick as I could and went straight at him. I didn't hesitate for a second. You should have seen me – even better still, you should have seen his face. He looked scared and confused. I went berserk. Like a mad woman. Screaming and yelling and clawing and kicking and punching at him. I didn't stop, not for a second. And it worked. He just looked totally confused. Then the bastard took off."

"Do you think you'd be able to give us a description?" asked Jensen.

"Definitely," said Catherine. "I'll never forget his face, ever."

CHAPTER TWENTY-TWO

As well as forensic evidence, we now had a description and photofit of the suspect.

With the surveillance operation deemed a disaster by Chief Webster, Fuller was keen to consider a new approach.

"We're going to split into two teams and start going door-to-door," said Fuller to the room of assembled officers. "If the Regent's Park Ripper is local, which psychological profiling and logic suggest he is, then our job is to flush him out. Everyone here has been given a photofit and a map. Anyone who hasn't got either the photofit or the map, go and see DS Jensen before leaving."

Fuller continued. "Someone out there knows who this man is and where he is. As soon as we start showing the picture around we need to be ready to respond. Stay on your toes and let's get a result. I'm now going to hand you over to DS Jensen."

Jensen stepped up to the front of the room. "I'm

going to head up Alpha group, and DCI James Hardy, who I'm sure needs no introduction, will be heading up the Beta group. As you arrived, you were all designated either group Alpha or group Beta. I don't need to stress to anyone here just how important it is we get this killer off our streets. He will kill again if not apprehended. So I want no mistakes. Hopefully, what we are aiming to achieve here today is easy enough to understand. Now, Detective Chief Inspector Hardy has something to say."

The room fell silent as all eyes turned to me. I let the silence hang in the air for a few seconds. Fuller and Jensen had done a good job of briefing everyone; there was now a sense of purpose and positivity, spirits were high and everyone was keen to get on with the job. My job was to make sure everyone knew who they were confronting.

"Many of you know me and the kinds of cases I work. Somehow, over the years, I've found myself working cases that, to a large extent, consist of brutal and often multiple homicides. I never chose those cases. Rather, it seems they chose me. And this has meant that I've spent a large part of my time on the force studying and pursuing and, fortunately, for the most part, arresting individuals with psychopathic tendencies. Individuals like the man you and I are tracking today. Individuals who consider their murderous acts a game.

"I want to make something perfectly clear: the level of violence this man is prepared to inflict on another human being makes him extremely dangerous, and not just to women. If he feels cornered and you're in his way, he will not hesitate to go through you. Don't doubt that for one second.

"You may know I lost a friend to this killer, and because of that I want him caught more than most, but not at any cost. I want you all to make it home safely tonight. You hear me? Be careful out there today. Look out for one another, watch each other's backs. We're going after a killer who has nothing to lose by harming any one of us."

Fuller wrapped things up and the room started to empty. "Let's go flush him out," he said. "Let's go get him."

He turned to me. "You might need to work on the motivational speaking a bit. I think you scared the life out of them." He slapped me on the back and walked ahead, chuckling to himself.

"Ignore him," said Jensen. "You did the right thing. They needed to hear the dangers."

CHAPTER TWENTY-THREE

I felt a true sense of pride as I looked at the huge turnout of officers. Everyone was keen to be involved. I'd learned some officers had given up their day off to be a part of what we were doing. There was a real sense of positivity in the air, and it felt good to be part of it.

Fuller coordinated from a temporary command post while Jensen and I insisted on being part of the team on the ground.

We went door-to-door, street-to-street, showing the picture and talking to everyone we met. As the minutes and hours passed, it felt like we were hunting a ghost. With each "*No*" and every shake of the head, I couldn't help feeling a more desperate need to catch a break. As morning became afternoon with not a single solid lead to show for it, I worried my confidence had been misplaced. But we kept at it, and finally, as our teams swept across town, our efforts slowly began to bear fruit. A few nods and distant recollections of possibly recognising the face. Hands went up and fingers pointed in the direction where he'd last been seen. I prayed we were closing in on the killer's home turf.

The smell of oil and petrol hit my nostrils as I entered J. B. Autocare.

"Hello. How can I help?" asked an older man at the front desk. With a puzzled expression, he looked behind me for my car.

"I'm looking for a man called Jim Bowers," I said. I introduced myself and showed him the picture of our suspect. "We're hoping he or you might have seen this man."

"I'm Jim Bowers," said the man, wiping his hands on his overalls. He took the picture, then squinted at it more closely and called a younger man over. "This is my son Mark," Bowers told me, then handed Mark the photo. "What do you think, Mark? Do you think it's him?"

"Could be," said Mark. "Same weasel eyes." He stepped away and went back inside the van he'd been working on.

Jim looked at me and handed back the laminated picture. "He in trouble?"

"We've got a few questions. We think he might be able to help us," I said, half truthfully.

"That'll be why there's an army of you out there?" Bowers looked over my shoulder at the constables knocking on doors across the street. "Is he the one that done those two women in the park?"

"What makes you say that?"

"No reason. Just putting two and two together and coming up with five."

His son laughed from inside the van.

I was getting impatient but didn't want Bowers clamming up on me. "Speaking to this man could lead to us catching whoever did murder those two young women. One of the women was the mother of a baby, only ten months old."

Bowers scratched the back of neck while he thought about what to say next. He called over his shoulder to his son, "What do you think?"

"Yeah, tell him. I never liked him anyway."

Bowers wiped his nose on the back of his wrist. "It could be Shane. Shane Colewell."

"It's definitely Weasel Boy," called Mark. "I'd put money on it."

My heart was thumping out of my chest. "How do you know him?"

"He worked here for a while, part-time, doing this and that. We had the idea of taking him on full-time, you know, training him up. It didn't work out. He was good with his hands. In fact, I still think he would have made a half-decent mechanic. But his heart wasn't in it. Don't ask me why. I think he had problems at home. Something just wasn't right."

"In what way?" I asked, trying to a get a feel for Colewell.

"Can't really put my finger on it. His attitude, maybe? Lack of commitment, I guess you could say. When he was given a task he'd do it, no problem. Other times, he'd just sort of drift off. Sometimes when you were talking to him, you could tell he was thinking about something else. He was a bit of a dreamer, I suppose. In the end we just decided he was the wrong fella to invest in. The weird thing was, when I told him things weren't going to work out, he didn't seem to mind. He just sat over there for the whole of the rest of the day." Bowers pointed to a torn and filthy old chair. "Then at the end of the day, when we clocked off, he clocked off with us. Natural as you like. He never came back, and we haven't seen him since."

"Do you know where I might find Colewell now?"

Bowers shrugged then stepped outside to the pavement and pointed to a block of flats. "Last I heard he was living with his mum in those flats over there on Augustus Street. Dunno if he's still there."

I looked at the flats and knew from experience if we started asking around on an estate like that, someone would tip him off.

"Any idea which number? I should imagine you'd have some sort of paperwork if he worked here."

Bowers looked at me as if he was regretting having opened his mouth. "Hang on."

He walked into a small, dirty office and flicked through piles of notes and receipts and delivery notes. He scratched his head, then tugged at a filing cabinet that was stuffed so full it couldn't be completely closed. He waved a scrap of paper in the air and stuck his head out through the office doorway. "Forty-two."

From inside the van Mark shouted, "If it was that weasel that murdered those women, tell your mates down the station to give the bastard a slap from me. And I mean a proper kicking."

His request rang in my ears as I hurried out of the garage and down the street. I pulled out my phone and hit Fuller's number.

CHAPTER TWENTY-FOUR

Fuller answered on the first ring.

"I've got a lead. Look into the name Shane Colewell. I'm headed over to his last known address, the flats on Augustus Street, flat number forty-two. You got that?"

"Yeah. You want backup?"

"I'll follow this up myself. No point putting anyone else onto this. For all I know, this might be a dead end. Keep everyone going door-to-door. I'll call if I get anything solid."

"What about Jensen?"

"Let her know and tell her I'll call her if I need her." I was sprinting now, dodging pedestrians and avoiding traffic. "I gotta go. I'll call when I know something."

I looked up at the block of flats while I caught my breath. Across the entrance to the flats a large group of youths were gathered, and I had clearly caught their attention. As I got closer the group started to melt away. They'd had no trouble determining I was police.

While most of the group watched from a distance,

one lad hopped up on the wall and sat staring at me. He'd decided he was going to stand his ground. After all, this was his patch.

He shoved his hands in his jacket pockets and slouched. "All right?" he said. "Can I help?"

I looked down the street. "Perhaps you can. I suppose it depends. What's your name?"

"Everyone calls me Buzz."

"So, Buzz, do you live in the flats?"

Buzz looked at me down his nose. "Why do you want to know that? You some sort of perv?"

"I think you and your friends know I'm police. I'm a detective." I showed my warrant card.

"Gotta check these things. The streets ain't safe. Mother told me never to talk to strangers. You know how it is." Buzz was mocking me; he was as street smart as any kid I'd ever met.

"Believe me, I do know how it is. Your mother's a wise woman."

"You taking the piss, Detective Hardy? You better not be talking bad on my mother."

"You have my word."

"So, what do you want with these flats?" asked Buzz. Despite his efforts to hide it, I could tell Buzz was a smart kid. The rest of the group were slowly heading our way, and I thought it best to get what I needed before they returned. Once back in his gang he'd be less inclined to assist.

I showed Buzz the photo of Colewell. "He lives in those flats," I said, stating it as fact.

Buzz shrugged. "I don't think so," he mumbled.

"All I want to know is which flat. That's it. It's a lot of flats and a lot of stairs. I don't want to go up and down all those flights of stairs for no good reason. I'm not as young as I used to be. Which flat is his?"

"You think I'm some sort of grass?" Buzz looked over at his friends, who were getting closer. The group had stopped and were talking to a couple of lads on scooters, who were revving the motors to get my attention.

"You wouldn't be grassing. To my knowledge he hasn't done anything wrong," I lied. "I just need to speak to him."

"You know what?" said Buzz hopping off the wall. "I gotta go. I ain't never seen him before."

I knew I'd stick out like a sore thumb if I started walking around the flats in my white shirt, suit and polished shoes. I needed to go straight to the Colewells' front door.

I stepped back and gave Buzz some space. As he turned to walk away, I said, "Tell you what, tough guy. You help me out and I won't call in a half dozen squad cars and insist they check the pockets of you and your buddies over there for weed and inhalants. I'm guessing you don't want to be known as the one that earned you and your mates a trip to the station?"

Buzz looked at me, sized me up, and began making out like he had a choice. We both knew the truth, but I played along.

"He's on the end there." Buzz turned his back to his friends and pointed with his thumb. "Third floor. Facing us. Far end. Two or three from the stairwell. Now I gotta go."

"Thanks, Buzz. You've done a good thing. Your mother would be proud. I guarantee it."

Buzz smiled briefly then headed off to brag to his pals about how he'd faced down a Scotland Yard detective.

CHAPTER TWENTY-FIVE

Keeping the miserable patch of grass to my left, I followed a concrete path to doors that led to a stairwell. I took the stairs two at a time. On the third floor I looked left and then right. My lungs were heaving. *I might be about to meet him*, my head kept telling me over and over.

I reached the third-floor hallway and checked the number on the first door. It began with a 4. This must be the correct floor. I looked over the railing at the patch of grass below. Buzz and his friends were now spectators.

As I started towards number 42, a door at the other end of the passage opened. A skinny figure in a blue t-shirt, track-suit bottoms and trainers filled the doorway. Over his shoulder he carried a rucksack. He dropped it to the floor beside him, crouched, and started searching through it. He had his back to me. This could be him. I needed to close the gap between us before he turned.

I picked up the pace, checking door numbers as I

moved: 36, 38, 40... Yup, this must be him. I was desperate to see his face.

He stood now, pulled the key from the lock and dropped it back in his rucksack. Then he turned and looked my way. Our eyes locked. In an instant I knew it was him. He matched the photofit, with the addition of some serious scratches down the side of his face and a split lip, courtesy of Catherine Simmons.

I played the innocent.

"Excuse me," I said. "I'm looking for my auntie's place."

Colewell wasn't fooled for a second. In an instant he'd turned and sprinted to a second stairwell.

"Stop. Police!" I shouted, then called "Shane, it's not a good idea to run. Let's talk." The only sound I heard was his feet rapidly hitting the stairs as his head start increased. "Shit."

I started after him, pulling out my mobile phone and calling Fuller as I ran. "This is Hardy. Backup needed. Augustus Street flats. I'm in pursuit. It's him – I feel certain. Shane Colewell is the killer."

CHAPTER TWENTY-SIX

Colewell knew the area better than I did, so losing sight of him would be disastrous. He was down the stairs like lightning, and as I reached the bottom I could see he'd already crossed the grassy area and was hopping over the wall onto the pavement. The rucksack was gone. He must have stashed it.

Buzz and his friends were cheering and laughing as I reached the grass. "Come on Sherlock, you can do it. He's getting away. Get those knees up."

Colewell looked over his shoulder as he crossed the road and ran straight into one of the scooter lads, sending them both to the ground. The lad sat cursing and swearing, trying to shove his bike off himself as Colewell got back to his feet and headed down the road to a playground.

I was gaining on him as we crossed the park. His initial burst had drained him and he was slowing.

A group of lads on bikes were still following and shouting a mixture of obscenities and mock encouragement. They gave up the chase after I threatened them with causing obstruction.

Colewell ran through the playground and took a sharp right at the exit. On seeing a squad car, its sirens blaring, turn into the road he climbed over a garden wall. He scaled the side gate. I heard the thump and clatter as he landed awkwardly on bins on the other side.

I waved to the squad car and they carried on past us. They turned into the next road to cut Colewell off behind the house.

Instead of scaling the gate I kicked it open. I shoved the bins aside and was pleased to see Colewell limping.

"Give it up, Shane," I yelled. "You're really pissing me off."

He ignored me, pushed open the back gate and headed towards a building site.

Despite his limp, Colewell picked up the pace before sliding under a gap in the perimeter fence. Beyond were churned-up plots and piles of building materials surrounding six partially built homes.

I got down onto my back and slid under the fence. My jacket snagged and I heard it tear as I attempted to yank it free. Now I was even more pissed off.

When I looked up again, Colewell had vanished.

The squad car pulled up on the other side of the fence.

"I want this place surrounded," I shouted as an officer climbed out. "Get backup. Get a helicopter and get a dog unit. The suspect, Shane Colewell, mustn't get away. You got that?"

"Yes, sir."

"And make sure Colewell doesn't double back. I'm going to search the houses." I took off my jacket and threw it towards the fence. I rolled up my sleeves as I started towards the empty buildings.

In two rows of three, the houses were at various stages of completion. I checked the first house and could smell the cold, damp air that filled it. Internal stud walls were up and electrical cables poked through holes in the plasterboard.

I came out of the house and walked around to where the back garden would eventually be.

An electrician was rooting around in the back of his van. He looked up when he heard me approach.

"I'm a detective. Have you seen—?"

"He went in that one." The electrician pointed with a large crowbar. "He looked like one of them oiks from the estate. I was just about to go over there and tell him to clear off."

As I approached the front door I grabbed a short length of wood from a skip outside.

CHAPTER TWENTY-SEVEN

The house was silent. I leaned back outside and looked over at the electrician. He nodded and confirmed I was in the right house.

"Shane Colewell," I called out. "I'm Detective Chief Inspector James Hardy. I'm a Scotland Yard detective. I'm here to help you. To do that, I need you to come out and walk slowly towards me, with your hands where I can see them. Do you hear me, Shane?"

Silence.

"We need to talk, Shane. This whole area is teeming with officers and police dogs. I can already hear the police helicopter overhead. Can you hear it, Shane? It's important you and I talk."

My whole body was tense as feelings of frustration, anticipation and hate coursed through me. I was just a few feet away from the man who had so brutally ended Cerise's life. The thoughts of the fear and helplessness she must have felt in her final moments were like daggers driving me forward. I needed to be the one to bring Colewell in. It had to be me.

I listened again. Still silence.

My hand tightened on the length of wood as I checked the downstairs rooms. A small, incomplete kitchen and dining area.

Keeping my back to the wall, I checked the next room, which would become the lounge.

I looked at the staircase. The balustrade had not been fitted. I kept my back to the wall and listened for any sound of movement as I crept upstairs. The steps creaked.

On the landing a large window threw light on four doorways. No doors had yet been fitted.

Before moving forward, I turned and watched through the window as officers fanned out around the building site. The gates to the site had been opened and a couple of squad cars were moving along the fresh tarmac road.

"Whatever you're feeling, Shane, I can get you help," I said as I began checking each room. "What you've done, I understand." I held the short length of wood up with both hands as I moved to the last room. "You're not the first person to feel what you feel. We can talk about it. These emotions are distressing – I understand that."

I held my breath and charged into the last room. I turned left and then right.

Nothing.

The room was empty.

"Damn it." How could I have missed him? Had he slipped past me?

I was in what would eventually become the master bedroom. Through the large window I could see the tops of the trees in Regent's Park.

I allowed my breathing to relax as I wondered what my next move should be. I didn't relish calling Fuller and telling him I'd lost the prime suspect.

I let the piece of wood fall to the floor and opened the double windows. Jensen was below. I leaned out and shouted to her, "He's not here. Check the other houses. I must have the wrong one."

Jensen looked up, nodded and made a call as she waved to officers to start checking the other houses.

I stood in silence. I kicked the piece of wood across the room. It hit the wall with a thud.

A shuffling sound caught my attention. It stopped. Then a creak.

I walked silently and stood at the doorway. Above me was a loft hatch.

CHAPTER TWENTY-EIGHT

"You up there, Shane?" I peered into the darkness of the hatch.

I stepped closer. Nothing. I walked underneath and peered from the other side.

Colewell came swinging through the loft hatch, knocking me to the floor. I landed heavily. He tried to run past me and I grabbed his leg, bringing him down behind me. He kicked back, repeatedly hitting me in the face. I let go of his leg and we both got to our feet.

Colewell charged at me. I grabbed hold of him and we fell onto the unfinished floor. He was skinny but strong. He wriggled free and ran for the length of wood. I was getting to my knees as he brought down the first blow across my back. I slumped to the floor as he delivered more heavy blows. I knew I needed to move.

"So you think you know me?" spat Colewell. "You know nothing." He beat me again and again, across my back and legs. I covered my head with my arms. "Want to know how it felt for those filthy bitches? I'll show you."

I rolled over as he raised the wood for another punishing blow, preparing to bring it down on my head.

Jensen called from the front door to the house. "Hardy? Are you there? We've found nothing."

Colewell glanced towards her voice. I got to my feet and sprang at him, shoving him backwards across the room, pushing him with all I had towards the open window. His eyes widened and then narrowed as he glared at me. I kept moving him closer and closer to whatever was beyond the open window.

He dropped the wood and grabbed my shirt.

His legs hit below the window and I kept pushing. One hand let go of me as he grasped the window frame.

Clawing at my shirt, he looked me in the eye. "Don't let me go. I go, we both go."

I looked down through the window. For the first time I noticed the pile of broken bricks and splintered wood below.

"Why the hell not?" I spat.

"You can't. You're police. You're no judge and jury – bitch."

He had a smug look on his face that said he knew I wouldn't let him fall.

I lifted him higher. He let go of my shirt with the other hand and grasped the window frame by his fingertips. I could see they were slipping.

"Who's to say you didn't fall, Shane? An accident. Who would care? Anyone looking on would say I was trying to save you."

"You can't just push me out of a window – you can't."

"Who says I can't? One of those women was a friend of mine, you worthless piece of shit."

I knew he could see the fury in my eyes. He twisted his face around, looked down at the rubble and broken bricks below, then looked back up at me. His eyes were full of terror.

"Oh, fuck," he whispered.

CHAPTER TWENTY-NINE

As a mark of respect, Rosie's Tea Shop had been closed the week of the funeral. So many bouquets of flowers had been left by customers and well-wishers during the lead-up to it that Rosie had been forced to put up a sign of thanks and respectfully request donations to charity instead.

The evening before Rosie's reopened, I dropped by to see how she was doing. After we hugged, we chatted and made small talk. Rosie changed the water in the vases. The room was alive with flowers. She showed me some of the messages she'd received.

"She really brightened so many lives," said Rosie, tears in her eyes.

"She did," I agreed. "She'll be remembered as bright, energetic, loving and giving. And that laugh of hers…"

Behind the counter I noticed the addition of a small, discreetly placed photo of Ceri on the wall. She was smiling broadly, and it looked like she was at the seaside.

I made us both tea, and we sat down at one of the tables. Rosie took a packet of cigarettes from her coat.

"Wales was a long journey. These were my companions." She held the packet up and showed me. "I quit over twenty years ago, and I don't plan on allowing that bastard to be the cause of my starting again." She crushed the packet and threw it in the bin.

"Colewell's been formally charged," I said finally. Rosie winced at the mention of his name. "He's going away for life. I'll let you know when the trial starts; I'm guessing you'll be there?"

She nodded and then sipped her tea thoughtfully. "Prison's too good for someone like him. Why should he get to live out the rest of his life?"

For a few precious seconds I'd had his life in my hands. There was no way I could ever tell her why I was unable to let him fall; I didn't know, myself. A part of me agreed completely with what she said: he didn't deserve to walk this earth while Ceri and Julia couldn't. Another part of me had known I could never look at Faith, Alice, Monica or Rosie – or myself – ever again with a clear conscience if I had done what every cell in my body had screamed at me to do.

"Perhaps you're right. There's no punishment suitable for a monster like Colewell. I wish I could have done more, but I'm no judge and jury – I'm just a detective."

Rosie was about to say something but changed her mind. Instead, she lifted my hand and kissed it. She smiled and said simply, "Thank you, James. You've done enough."

THE DCI HARDY SERIES

KNIFE & DEATH

The body of a young college student is discovered in the River Thames, and DCI James Hardy is horrified to learn that the murdered woman was a family friend.

As he begins to investigate, he discovers that Anya, the victim's flatmate, is missing, seemingly on the run for her life. Realising that she could be the key to catching the killer, Hardy races against time to track down Anya before the killer does.

As the ugly truth behind the investigation unfolds, Hardy's own family come under threat. With two young daughters to protect and an investigation that twists and turns, frustrating him at every step, Hardy finds himself pushed to the limit.

Can he protect his family? Will Hardy be in time to save Anya? With his every move under scrutiny, how will Hardy handle the pressure and solve the investigation?

Available on Amazon.

ANGELS

Detective James Hardy's caseload is bursting at the seams. A serial murderer dubbed The Angel Killer is stalking young women in Hardy's new hometown, and an assassin is picking off high-profile political figures one by one, with his ultimate target being the prime minister herself.

Both cases land squarely on Hardy's desk even as he struggles to rebuild a stable home for himself and his two young daughters after the senseless murder of their mother.

As the body counts rise in both investigations and the killers become bolder and more confident, Hardy realises he needs to get his head in the game and put his personal life on hold once again, jeopardising the very stability he has fought so hard to create.

Set against an electrifying backdrop of political intrigue and chilling personal vendettas, *Angels* is an emotionally charged, harrowing examination of human nature and motivation, and the definition of evil itself.

Available on Amazon.

HARD TRUTH

After the brutal murder of his wife by a crazed drug-seeker, Detective Chief Inspector James Hardy walks away from his career as a Scotland Yard homicide detective. He has found love again, and, together with his two young daughters, he's making a fresh start in a small seaside town.

With his new career as a consultant taking off and the demons of the past behind him, Hardy's life couldn't be better.

But the peace is about to be shattered.

When a series of shocking murders take place in the seaside town, Hardy is contacted by local detective inspector Emma Cotton for advice. As Cotton investigates the killings, Hardy learns the disturbing crimes have all the hallmarks of a serial killer linked to his past.

The notorious Kelly Lyle, known as The Mentor, has surfaced again, and has Hardy and his family in her sights. As she embarks on her latest bloody campaign of murder and revenge, she rips apart the detective's new life – and reveals a dark secret that shatters everything Hardy believed to be true about his wife's death.

Hardy balks at being forced out of early retirement, but whether he likes it or not, the killer appears determined to draw him back into a world he wants to leave behind.

Knowing it will take something monumental to catch his attention, the killer raises the stakes and abducts someone Hardy loves more than life itself.

Is Hardy about to lose everything he's fought so hard to keep?

Hardy's only choice is to work with DI Emma Cotton to discover the hard truth behind the killer's motives. If they play the killer's game, they might be in time to stop a tragedy beyond comprehension.

Available on Amazon.

INFERNO

Searching for the truth,
means coming under fire.

DCI James Hardy was hoping for a quiet life. He stepped away from his career at New Scotland Yard and moved his family to the south coast to start over. For a short while, life was good. But now the past is catching up with him.

Hardy recently learned that Edward Fischer, aka Edward Richter, the man he arrested for a string of killings, is also the man who orchestrated his wife's murder. And now, Fischer has escaped from prison and is on the run.

Fischer is a free man, and before he leaves the country and disappears for good, he's looking for compensation from Hardy. The sort of compensation money can't buy. The kind that will cause Hardy pain and suffering.

And when Hardy's new home becomes a target and his family come under threat, he finds he has no choice but to step up and do what he's best at... catching killers.

Available on Amazon.

MORE DCI HARDY . . .

Want to hear what Jay's working on, and enjoy DCI Hardy bonus material?

I *occasionally* send newsletters, usually once a quarter. I talk about what I'm working on, new releases and other bits of news relating to the DCI James Hardy series.

It's easy to join my mailing list, and you won't get spammed (I promise):

1. Receive news, announcements and updates on new releases before anyone else.
2. Read a profile of DCI James Hardy called: Who is James Hardy? *(Exclusive to my mailing list, you can't get this anywhere else.)*
3. Access to bonus scenes from *every* book in the Hardy series: For example, you'll find out what happens to the nasty piece of work, Melvin Barclay - featured in Hard Truth - when Kelly Lyle catches up with him again. *It isn't pretty!* There is also a scene from INFERNO which has been described as taut and nerve-shredding. *(Exclusive to my mailing list, you can't get it anywhere else.)*

Sign up for updates at www.jaygill.net/newsletter

ABOUT JAY GILL

Born in Dorset, southern England, Jay Gill moved to Buckinghamshire where he worked in the printing industry, primarily producing leaflets and packaging for the pharmaceutical industry. After several years of the London commute, and with his first child about to start school, he realised it was high time for a change and moved back to the south coast of England. This change freed up time for him to write the detective stories he dreamed of one day publishing.

Safe to say, he's caught the writing bug in earnest now. With several DCI Hardy novels under his belt, a growing "family" of characters both good and heinous, and a host of exciting new ideas bouncing around in his head, Jay busily juggles his writing and family life and is hard at work on the next instalment in the DCI James Hardy series of thrillers.

SPREAD THE WORD

If you've enjoyed this book, please help spread the word by leaving a review on Amazon. It can be as short or as long as you like. Reviews help bring the DCI Hardy novels to the attention of other readers.

If you've never left a book review before, it's easy: simply write whatever is true for you – for example, your experiences as you were reading, your impressions of the characters, what you thought of the writing itself, and who else the story might appeal to. Your words will be a beacon of sorts for others like us, who love crime thrillers.

Many thanks, Jay

Made in United States
North Haven, CT
30 October 2022

26132322R00071